For John Taft Ingalls

Two fishes swimming in the sea,
Two birds flying in the air,
Two chisels on an anvil – maybe.
Beaten, hammered, laughing blue steel to each other – maybe.
Sure I would rather be a chisel with you
                                    than a fish.
Sure I would rather be a chisel with you
                                    than a bird.
Take these two chisel pals, O God.
Take and beat'em, hammer 'em,
                        hear 'em laugh.

"Laughing Blue Steel" by Carl Sandburg

MOVING HEAVY

THINGS

Written and Illustrated by
JAN ADKINS

ISBN: 0-395-29206-9 Lib. of C. Card No. 80-464 PAP ISBN 0-395-60284-x
RNF BP PB SEM 10 9 8 7 6 5 4

BEGINNINGS

An ant. There is one here, twiddling mindlessly across my desk, carrying a crumb of enormous proportions. It is a crumb of whole wheat bread from my sandwich and I hope he enjoys it, but it is bigger than the ant by three or four times.

A powerful creature. If I were as strong as the ant, proportionally, I could throw grand pianos, carry drums of oil in either hand, lift cars out of their parking spaces, uproot respectable trees, and pick up between 1500 and 2000 pounds of whole wheat bread. I would be a comic book hero who didn't need a car jack, a fork lift, or a moving van.

None of us is as strong as the ant, nor do we need to be. It's possible for most of us to live out our lives without lifting anything heavier than the Sunday paper. We come to identify weight with motors and machinery: if there is a heavy thing to be moved, a machine is called in; its motor bawls, its cylinders hiss, its wheels squeal, and the thing is moved.

Simple, fast, and complete, and that's the way things are.

There was a time when things weren't moved in that way. It was not so long ago, half a hundred years, just before engines came to be small and cheap and everywhere. Most older folks remember how it was. It was a time when elm logs were burned and bored out to make water conduit, and if you could step back in time to suggest that they use cast iron pipe they would laugh at you, and be right to laugh: "Listen here, Basil, fellow here says we ought to use water pipe cast in . . . what? Iron? Iron, Basil. Yup, that's what he says. Maintains that some poor jasper ought to mine the ore, then it gets shipped to the smelter and cast into pigs, the pigs get to the foundry somehow and get reheated and cast into pipe. Then the railroad brings those big pipes to the depot and you and I'd have to manhandle them into place. Think of the human labor, all the fuel, ship and rail and horse transport as against you and me cutting elm down the road and shaping it up and boring it and laying it right here and it lasts just as long, elm

does, maybe longer. Why, that's just foolish. What about that, Basil?"

It may be that your life has a few heavy things in it. You may be more than a match for the Sunday *Times,* but, if you have occasions for moving on a more formidable scale, you could yell for a fork lift and throw in the towel, or you could be stubborn and prideful. Machines, or the oil they burn, could go against your grain, or you might have a practical turn of mind like Wallace and Basil when they reason that elm conduit is simpler and more direct than cast iron. It may seem to you that moving a heavy thing with some application of leverage or

guile can be set up and accomplished before the machines would arrive, without the expense of oil or dollars. It may suit your pride or your parsimony or your humor, or it may suit that rare sense of rightness that comes when you use just enough hammer for the nail, salt for the soup, charcoal for the steak, or string for the package . . . and no more.

Prompted by vanity, necessity, or convenience, your intention of moving some weighty mass may be stopped dead when you confront the thing itself, silently glaring at you, defiant and heavy. How do you approach it? How do you begin?

Wallace and Basil had it easier. In their day no one

5

expected a fork lift or a front loader to drive up for a hundred years. Every community had the tools and the know-how to get the job done. Basil would fetch rollers from Niedemeyer's barn while Wallace conferred with local riggers to see if they had pulled off a similar piece of work. It was likely they had. As for you, the tools are simple, and you can be encouraged by the accomplishments of hands that did their work long ago: the idea that Stonehenge and the pyramids of Egypt and the Americas couldn't have been done without the unidentified fork lifts and flying backhoe saucers of space travelers is an insult to the Pharaohs and their architects, to the mysterious Druids, to the merciless emperor Chin and his Great Wall, to the master builders of Angkor Wat, Rome, Rheims, and to Wallace and Basil.

You begin, then, with confidence that it can be done and no doubt *has* been done. You can unstick a car, move a piano, install a refrigerator, haul a boat, hoist an engine, or carry a friend. Toward your beginning, here are some kindergarten basics, a primer of moving.

Precept One:

There's more than one way to skin a cat.
It can be done, allright, probably in several ways. The process usually is selecting the *best* solution. Complicated problems can be easier to solve because they have six or eight ways to get around behind them, whereas simple problems with one impossible solution can be the very devil . . . until you step back and find *their* back door.

Precept Two:

The Geezer Ploy
When the old fellows didn't have diesel cranes to pull their fat out of the fire, they were obliged to be fiendishly clever. Ask yourself how they would have set up for your problem in 1900, in 1800, 1700, and so forth.

Precept Three:

The Aristotelian Approach

In short, think about it. You are stronger than the ant because you use your mind to increase the utility of your muscles. Enthusiasm is essential, but an hour of sitting on your duff thinking about the problem can be worth two hours of sweating out a rash plan. Look at your problem, touch it all over, let it speak to you, draw it out on paper.

Precept Four:

A Friend in Need

Get yourself a big, powerful friend, several if possible. Yes, yes, this book does celebrate brain over brawn, but sometimes you've just got to have a big hulk behind a long lever to make it all work. Working alone can be surprisingly effective but it's lonely; work goes faster with help, and teamwork is an awesome force. It is also true that working alone with heavy, unwieldy loads can be purely dangerous.

Precept Five:

Applied Sloth

As stated in the stagehand's axiom: "Never lift what you can drag, never drag what you can roll, never roll what you can leave." Creativity germinates in indolence, and the cleverest people are often the laziest: they are always looking for an easier way. The easiest way is often the simplest, most direct, and the best way.

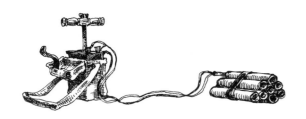

Precept Six:

The Sum of the Parts Stratagem

Must your load be moved in one lump sum? It is occasionally effective to disassemble here and reassemble there. This usually violates the next precept, but it's a viable consideration.

Precept Seven:

The Power of Simplicity

The more complex a machine or procedure or set-up becomes, the less directly it applies its power. Simple forces applied intelligently should carry the day. (If not, see precept one.) This is no snub of wile or cleverness or inventiveness, only a caution against dissipating your efforts in the bother and friction of complication.

Precept Eight:

The Power/Time Tradeoff

It is a principle of machines that the long throw of a lever's arm applies a greater force at the shorter arm, but over a shorter throw. A small, fast-turning gear drives a large gear: the larger gear's shaft will turn with more power, but more slowly. Similarly, the power of blocks & tackle, chain drives, wedges, and screws can be increased by reducing their throw. The lesson here is that you can lift an enormous weight if you are content to lift it just a little; you can move anything if you've got the time. Time is relative; so is strength.

Precept Nine:

Softly, Softly, Catchee Monkey
Don't swoop. Lift and move in small, orderly, safe stages. Set reasonable goals. Step by step the longest march is won. Sprinters burn out and drop things.

Precept Ten:

Murphy: 3 – Home Team: 0
Murphy's Law in its simplest form, *"If something can go wrong, it will,"* is interpreted by some to be part of the law of entropy, by some to be doom-saying gloom, by others to be good sense. It has a volume of corollaries. For our purposes these are the critical passages: *"If there is a crucial point or time for a failure, that's where or when it will occur,"* and *"Any failure will occur so as to do the most damage."* The odds of failure can be calculated roughly thus: *"The odds of the bread falling jam-side down are proportional to the cost of the carpet."* The lessons of Murphy's Law are: don't put your hand under it unless you've got it blocked; get the Ming vase out of the room, all the way out; absolute faith in any piece of equipment is absolute folly; expect disaster and have a back-up plan to minimize it; be careful.

Precept Eleven:

Stability

Just as important as lifting or moving heavy things is keeping them from falling over. Consider it through every step of your plans. Consider an object's center of balance, never letting it stray outside or even near the base of its support. Use gravity for you, thinking in terms of stable pyramids with broad bases. Remember that a triangle is the only inherently stable construction.

Precept Twelve:

The Beached-Whale Caution

Out of water a whale's lungs cannot support its massive bulk and it dies for lack of breath. Many heavy things will not support their own weight in some attitude: on their backs, upside down. It may be necessary (and easier) to move some things on a pallet, supports, or in a cradle. Boats out of water are notably delicate: just as you cannot bend a line to a grand piano's back leg and hoist away, you cannot haul a boat haphazardly. Misplaced supports can be pushed through a boat's hull by its own weight. Every piece should be given careful consideration before placing the lines or supports that will carry it.

Precept Thirteen:

What Goes up Comes down Heavier
The refrigerator you push up the stairs without too much trouble takes a lot of stopping once it gets up a little momentum going down. Lowering weights from heights puts more strain on the tackle and the line and the poor sod holding it than lifting weights. Momentum is a force with which to reckon.

Precept Fourteen:

The Best Laid Plans of Mice and Men Gang Aft A-gley.
Anything you botch you can fix. If you start any job with the fear of making a single misstep you might as well forget it: you will not work smoothly, you will be hesitant and nervous. If ("when," see Precept Nine) it goes wrong, you can work another plan. Relax. Leave perfection to watchmakers.

Precept Fifteen:

The Phantom Run-through
Picture your plan, picture it ready to go and set up in every way, then walk it through, visualizing how the path fits the piece, the lifts and the let-downs, the tight places and the rest stops. Ask yourself what tools you will need, where Murphy's Law can raise its head, and how you can do it better.

Precept Sixteen:

How Much Fixing Will the Fix Take?
What are the side effects? Will rollers scratch the floor? Is this plan too risky? Can you accomplish anything without moving something heavy? (Does that cat *have* to be skinned?) Is it worth it? Could a crane or fork lift or backhoe or trave-lift do it cheaper in the long run?

THE BODY

As you begin this business of moving heavy things you should know that you have a disadvantage: your body. To move loads well you should be built something along the lines of an elephant: something sensibly founded on four feet with enormous strength and enough weight to anchor it, a pair of ivory lift bars, a prehensile crane, a push-bar forehead, and scuff-resistant skin. The body you've got there is designed as a multipurpose tool with the advantages and limitations of diversity. We walk on two feet, and this has allowed us to use our hands as specialized tools (precise if delicate), but standing erect exposes our weakest part – our spine – to forces that can harm it.

Picture your body as three parts: At the bottom, your legs, your strongest asset, based on feet that can adjust to a good range of angles to keep everything fairly stable; at the top, a heavy assembly of head and shoulders with arms for grasping and pushing;

12

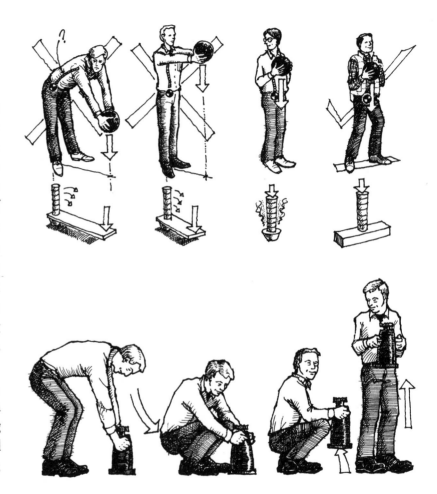

between them, your flexible, vulnerable spine, like a stack of nesting cups fastened together with a string through the bottoms. Picking up a bowling ball can be a safe or a dangerous lift: leaning out and using your back to lift is placing an unfair strain on your vertebrae and the pads of cartilage between them. Even holding a weight away from your body strains the column of bones that is so easily damaged and so long in healing. Bring the load in to you, hug it as close to your own center of gravity as you can, and use your legs and feet to make a stable base.

When you pick up a load off the floor, use a safe routine. Swing your rump down with the first strain and use your elbows against your thighs to lever the load up and to you; now use your legs and come up without any strain on your back. Your body will do what you tell it to do and it has no automatic governors, so you can do your own body damage, make no mistake about that. It is not uncommon for rowers and runners and weightlifters to tear muscles, ligaments, to crush cartilage, even to break their own ribs.

Play to your strengths. The strongest forces you can exert are in your legs, especially during the last stage of straightening them. The last five or six inches of straightening and rising slightly on the balls of your feet are powerful. You can usually work a lift to utilize those inches. Your arms are more powerful pulling than pushing because your pulling biceps are more developed than your pushing triceps, and this is another advantage to use.

Good body lifts play to strengths. The dead-man's carry really requires a standing body and a deft bit of balancing to tuck head and shoulder into the abdomen of the person to be carried, then to use the momentum of the body slumping over to straighten and rise *with the legs*. Practice this on soft grass a few times and you'll be able to lift even larger people safely and securely. The two-person carry is a simple matter of interlocking hands and forearms.

The weight in a modern pack, like this Jansport D-5, is carried directly on the hips with a padded

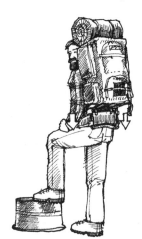

belt; the back and shoulders stabilize the load but take little strain. A traditional carry for canoeists is a Duluth pack with a tumpline that carries the load on the forehead and back; this is a workable system but it takes some training.

Movers' straps are strips of canvas or burlap or leather that hold the load as the mover uses that powerful few inches of leg to lift it. They are used in many ways: here, as a tumpline tensioned by wrists and arms, and as a simple backstrap twisted tight and held in this simple twistknot by the hands. A strong, seasoned mover can even carry a piano.

The porter's knot is a head cushion made by turning a large bandanna back into its own twist. Though it takes some experience, it is a good carry for bulky loads and is used all over the world. Slinging a tiger or a trunk to a pole and sharing the load is a traditional, useful carry.

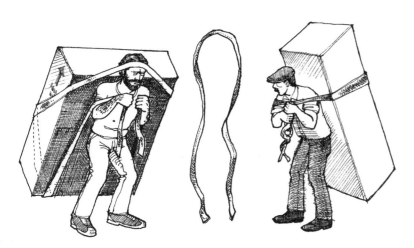

In the autumn of 1880 a stone pier was to be built to reach out from Indian Neck in Wareham, Massachusetts, but the stone sloops beating down from Cheabague, Maine, could not approach that beach. They were too deep in the water. The great blocks of rough granite were off-loaded at the channel inside the Neck and laid in orderly rows. Late that fall a shallow trench was dug around the Neck, using the moon tide high-water line as a level mark. In February of 1881, when the Neck and Upper Buzzards Bay were frozen, the trench was sprinkled with warm water, which froze quickly. When it had been sprinkled many times, the trench formed a level track of ice over which the granite blocks were skidded quickly and easily. That spring and summer the pier was built. The Indian Neck pier is a lesson in moving heavy things: the builders were patient and ingenious, using natural forces and

Winter 1881

intelligence over brute force and solving their
problems simply, directly, with the least effort.
Their first problem was the mover's prime obstacle:
friction.

Autumn 1880

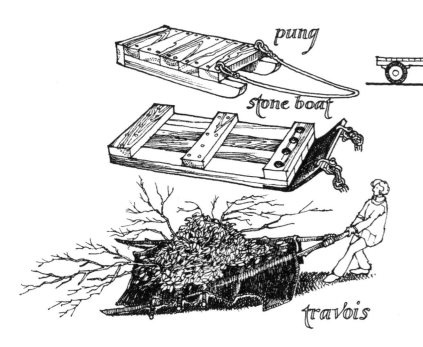

pung

stone boat

travois

FRICTION

When suspended in deep space an object, once moving, continues to move at the same rate forever. Nothing stops it. Here on earth the problem is weightier.

Two traditional tools for reducing friction are the *pung,* a sled for dirt or grass or snow, and the *stone boat,* a smooth, flat surface. They still have advantages over wheeled carts. Axles and bearings need space, and small wheels can't climb over small obstacles and tend to sink into soft surfaces (wagons and carts, therefore, are usually higher). A load can often be rolled directly onto the low beds of pungs

18

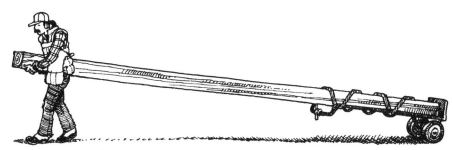

and stone boats. These old load-movers are simple, and can be knocked together on the site, and can sometimes negotiate rough surfaces more easily.

The *travois* is an ancient answer to friction, and can still be helpful in the garden. A *tarpaulin* can haul a grand load of light leaves, and a big cardboard carton slicked up with dance-floor wax will slide heavy loads just as a square of carpet on a waxed floor will. Winter subverts friction: snow and ice are useful, especially with a *toboggan* or a junk car hood. Water was used in narrow farm canals and iceways to move considerable loads. If you can stabilize the load, any slippery surface or set of wheels will make the going easier.

19

The cunning ways friction has been reduced would please the great Leonardo da Vinci. Monument builders move marble, granite, and slate blocks on their bases with ice cubes, adjusting positions and then allowing the unwieldy weights to melt into place. Sheet metal workers move half-ton flats of sheet copper and stainless steel by levering them up and rolling baseballs beneath them. Similarly, mausoleums roll coffins into vaults with marbles: simple, expendable. Air can be used to slide loads: hovercraft cross the English Channel with hundreds of passengers, cars, and trucks; plywood can be drilled and epoxy-fitted with hose fittings, then elevated (about 1/16″) with an air compressor to make a sliding pallet; gym mats are moved by flipping one edge to force a cushion of slippery air under it.

Professional movers are never far from a hand truck, and every construction site has a fleet of wheelbarrows. One of the most useful movers for house and garden is the Gardenway cart whose big wheels, axled toward the middle rather than one end, make heavy loads easy to handle (though you must load the bed systematically to prevent its tipping over).

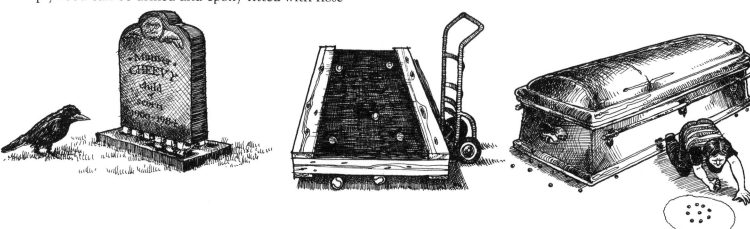

There is always one more way to skin a cat. Jay Baldwin, technical editor of *Co-Evolution Quarterly*, tells of a boatbuilder who proudly announced to Jay that he had *not* built his boat too big to bring out of his garage; he had allowed a full ½″ top and sides. Jay could not imagine how they could put wheels or rollers under the boat in half an inch. Oh. The boat came smoothly out . . . on bacon rinds. It was so well lubricated that it slid down the driveway and into the street.

In northern waters we are obliged to haul our boats out of the water each year, lest ice abuse our

single wheel is tippy but can roll on a **plank** *across a gap or mud.*

runners *behind the wheels, in some cases moving treads, make climbing and descending stairs smoother.*

moved forward as the beam reaches its balance point

stationary rollers

hulls. A boat out of water is like a duck in the desert: out of place and pitifully vulnerable. Hauling is a nervous time for any boat owner.

A cradle made for the boat is weighted with scrap iron and rolled into the water. The cradle rests and moves on rollers of iron pipe (easier to use at any depth because they sink) or wood, which bear on a "track" of planking that presents a smooth, hard surface to the rollers.

When the boat is guided into position on its cradle, a delicate teamwork comes into play. Teams on either side check each roller for alignment,

tapping the ends with sledges to set them true. They shout their approval and call for a "bid" – a careful move of one or two feet. Just before the bid, each team pulls the chocks they have tucked under the downhill side of the rollers; a truck winch provides the pulling power. When the bid is made, the chocks are slipped back into place.

As the boat comes out of the water and settles its dead weight on the cradle, attention is given to assure a close fit between boat and cradle. Bid by bid, the boat moves up the sand, the rollers crossing from one track plank to another. Finally the cradle

22

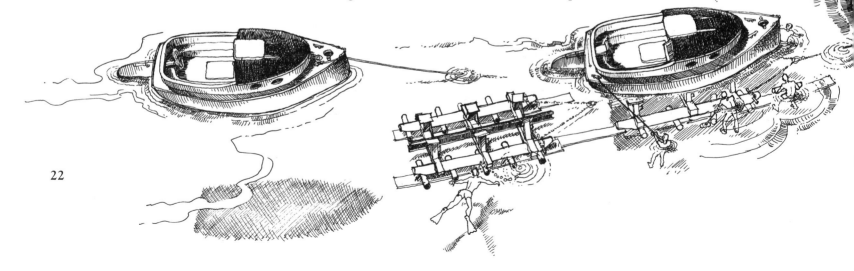

is jacked up, one side at a time, and the rollers removed. The catboat can be put to bed for a long, raw winter.

Rollers, the oldest wheels, have been moving heavy things since the first foot rolled out from under its owner on a smooth, round stick. Rollers

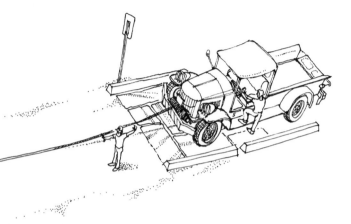

are simple, strong, adaptable, cheap, and compact, and can be used under any even surface. You can set up rollers in situations where a wheel-and-axle vehicle isn't available or doesn't fit, and where water or weight would damage a more complicated carriage.

Building a cradle for a boat, or for any beached-whale risk, makes moving simpler. The *riders* take the strain of towing and rollers; their raked ends

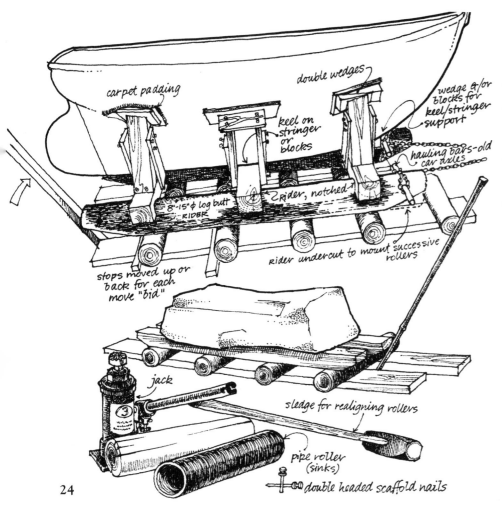

carpet padding

double wedges

wedge &/or blocks for keel/stringer support

keel on stringer or blocks

hauling bars-old car axles

Rider, notched

8"-15"∅ log butt RIDER

Rider undercut to mount successive rollers

stops moved up or back for each move "bid"

jack

sledge for realigning rollers

pipe roller (sinks)

double headed scaffold nails

24

make a ramp for rollers of slightly different sizes and provide for deflection due to weight. The *stringers*, set with bolts or drift pins into the notched riders and braced with horizontal diagonals, take the weight; blocks and wedges are used to give as much bearing surface as possible and to equalize the load. (An experienced mover has some notion of load from the resistance and "feel" of blocks and wedges

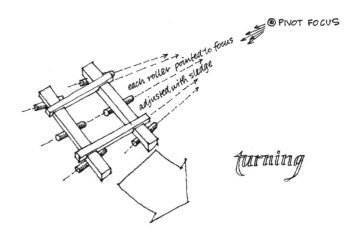

PIVOT FOCUS

each roller pointed to focus adjusted with sledge

turning

and rollers as he taps them home with a sledgehammer.) The side supports, or *poppets*, take some weight and stabilize the load; they angle out and are braced diagonally; and they are shimmed and padded where they meet the hull for maximum bearing surface. Cradles are often made on the spot using an existing set of riders and stringers, and the temporary poppets are fastened with scaffold nails.

Moving is a careful, measured march of individual bids in which the difference is apparent between *static friction*, the resistance to be overcome before moving starts, and *dynamic friction*, the lesser resistance to continuous motion. A bid is started with a strong nudge from levers and continued with the winch.

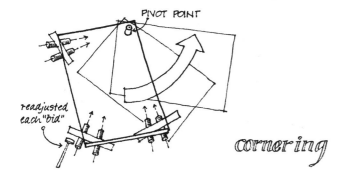

readjusted each "bid"

PIVOT POINT

cornering

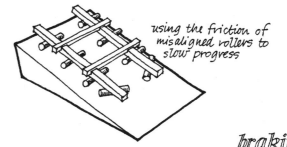

using the friction of misaligned rollers to slow progress

braking

LINE

At its best, strong, tense, portable, versatile; at its worst, a confusing bewilderment with a persistent and even malevolent tendency to catch and tangle.

Basic linework is simple good sense. First, keep your line in usable condition: dry (especially natural fibers), away from sunlight (especially synthetics), and in a loose, orderly, clockwise coil without tangles, hockles (twisted separations of the strands), or knots. When handling a live load, *take a turn*: one or more turns around a post or cleat or pin or any sturdy device uses friction to cut the load considerably, allowing one person to hold or slack off tremendous pull. Taking a turn is important when *making fast* (tying off an end): when a line is loosed it may be under strain, and the turns let you release the load slowly and safely.

Putting a strain on a line or tightening a line is a cautious operation. Without machinery you can exert destructive forces that can part the line or

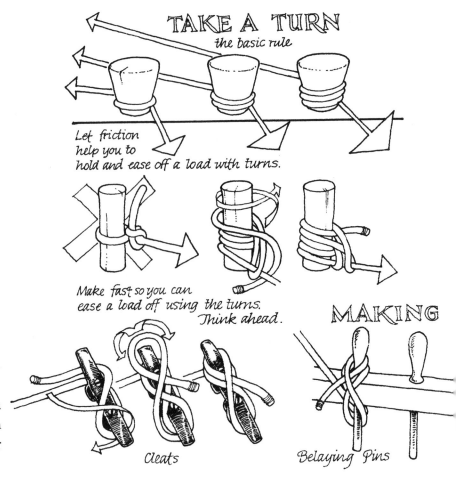

TAKE A TURN
the basic rule

Let friction help you to hold and ease off a load with turns.

Make fast so you can ease a load off using the turns. Think ahead.

Cleats

MAKING

Belaying Pins

26

break equipment. *Swigging* uses side pulls on the line to multiply forces; one hand leans out with the line and swings down hard with the resulting slack while another hand *tailing on* takes up the slack around a cleat or post. Other methods use twisting or a crude block & tackle formed with the line itself, but note that sharp turns always weaken line.

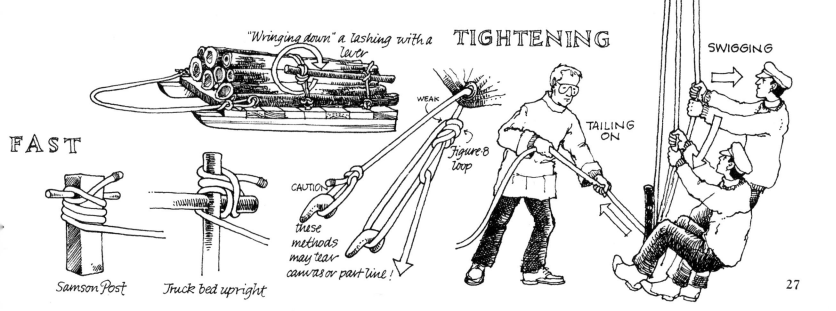

"Wringing down" a lashing with a lever

TIGHTENING

SWIGGING

WEAK

Figure-8 loop

TAILING ON

FAST

Samson Post

Truck bed upright

CAUTION

these methods may tear canvas or part line!

You could do a lifetime's linework if you mastered the dozen knots here and learned how to use them. *Hitches* attach lines to things: the *clove hitch,* shown over a cylinder and a bollard, is for pull away from an object; the *rolling hitch* is for lengthwise pull; the *ring* hitch attaches a line to a ring or small-diameter rod; and the *cow hitch* secures a middled line or a loop and can be another good ring hitch with additional turns. The *bowline* is one of the most useful knots and should be practiced to quick perfection. The

clove hitch　　　　　　*rolling hitch*

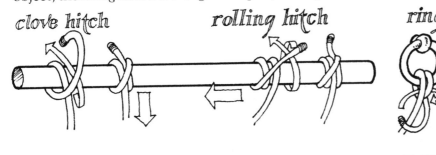

ring hitch　　　*cow hitch*

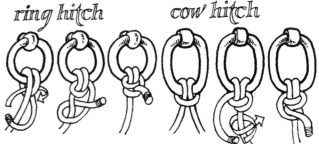

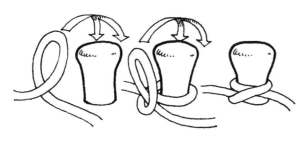

KNOTS

bowline　　　　　　　　　　　　　*figure 8*

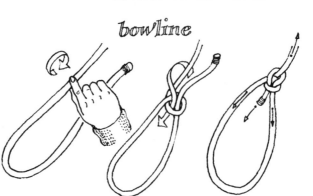

28

figure eight is a *stopper knot* that prevents a line from running through a hole. *Bends* attach lines to lines: the *sheet bend* is a variation on the bowline, the *becket bend* is for mating large lines to small lines, and the *carrick bend* is the most secure and workable

of the bends. The *reef knot,* sometimes called the *square knot,* is for *binding,* like the *constrictor knot,* which is powerful but stubborn to untie. The *lineman's loop* is a secure, nonjamming loop ideal for a shoulder harness along a long line.

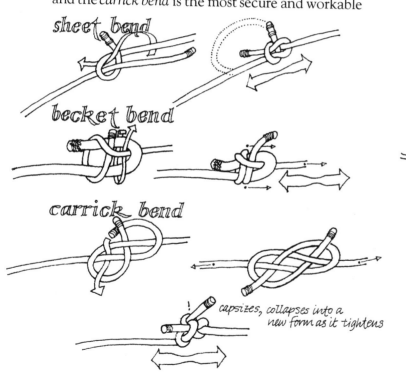

sheet bend

becket bend

carrick bend

capsizes, collapses into a new form as it tightens

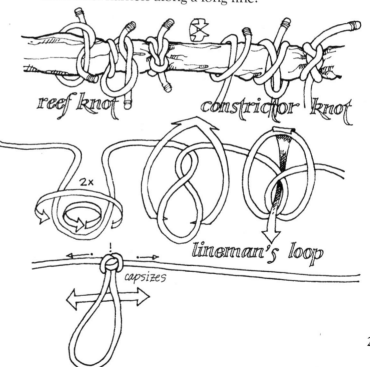

reef knot   *constrictor knot*

2×

lineman's loop

capsizes

A line suspending a weight is a simple problem in tension, but hanging a weight by two angled lines brings other forces into play. Run a cord through the handle of an iron skillet and let it hang down between your hands. The straighter you make the cord the harder you must pull. The tension in the line grows and its tendency to pull out of your hands grows with it. When you are lashing down a load for lifting, pay attention to the angles.

The *rope sling* is easy to splice up; the *flour sling* of

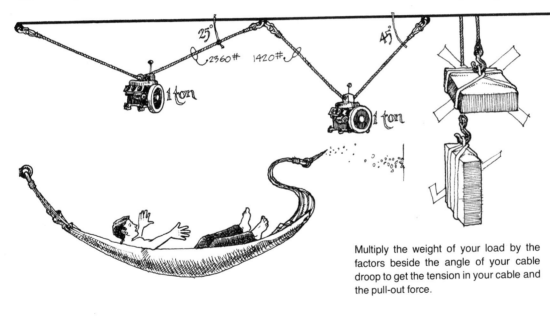

ANGLES

<°	tension	pull-out
90°	.5	0
80°	.51	.10
70°	.53	.18
60°	.58	.29
45°	.71	.50
30°	1.00	.87
25°	1.18	1.07
20°	1.46	1.37
15°	1.93	1.86
10°	2.88	2.83
5°	5.74	5.72

Multiply the weight of your load by the factors beside the angle of your cable droop to get the tension in your cable and the pull-out force.

rope and heavy canvas distributes the load; the *selvagee strop* made up of coiled rope yarn half-hitched together is a nonslip sling.

Because of sudden jerks, inequalities of rope, and Murphy's Law, the *working load* of a line is one-sixth or even one-seventh of the *breaking load,* and the working load is halved if the line is knotted in any way. Gloves are advisable if you are handling loads with rope, essential if you are handling cable, whose occasional wild wires can rip your hand open.

LINE STRENGTH

0"	manila	dacron	dacron braid	nylon	nylon braid	cable† gal 7x19
3/16"	406* / 70+	900 / 150	1040 / 170	900 / 150	1040 / 170	4200 / 840
1/4"	540 / 900	1500 / 250	1840 / 300	1490 / 250	1600 / 280	7000 / 1400
5/16"	900 / 150	2320 / 390	2870 / 480	2150 / 360	2700 / 450	9800 / 1960
3/8"	1220 / 200	3470 / 580	4140 / 690	3340 / 560	3800 / 630	14400 / 2900
7/16"	1580 / 260	4500 / 750	5630 / 940	4500 / 750	5200 / 870	17600 / 3500
1/2"	2380 / 390	5370 / 890	7360 / 1230	6100 / 1000	7200 / 1200	22800 / 4500
5/8"	3460 / 575	8100 / 1350	12,400 / 2000	9000 / 1500	12,600 / 2100	
3/4"	4860 / 810	11,150 / 1900	15,600 / 2600	13,600 / 2200	16,000 / 2700	
7/8"	6950 / 1160	16,100 / 2700	22,900 / 3800	20,000 / 3300	24,700 / 4100	
1"	8100 / 1350	20,400 / 3400	26,700 / 4500	26,200 / 4400	24000 / 4000	
1-1/4"	12200 / 2000		40,800 / 6800	36,200 / 6000	44,000 / 7400	
1-1/2"	16,700 / 2800		57,000 / 9500	63,000 / 10,500		

*breaking strength
+working load, calculated at one-sixth breaking load
†working load for cable is one-fifth breaking strength
‡diameter of the bar-stock

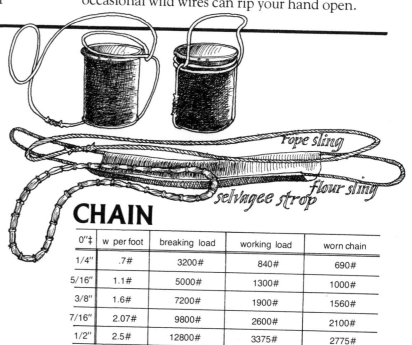

rope sling

selvagee strop   flour sling

CHAIN

0"‡	w per foot	breaking load	working load	worn chain
1/4"	.7#	3200#	840#	690#
5/16"	1.1#	5000#	1300#	1000#
3/8"	1.6#	7200#	1900#	1560#
7/16"	2.07#	9800#	2600#	2100#
1/2"	2.5#	12800#	3375#	2775#

BLOCK & TACKLE

Among the simplest machines. *The power/time trade-off* is evident in working with them: A *twofold purchase* runs through four feet of line for a one-foot gain, but the forces are multiplied by four. *The power of simplicity* is also apparent here in the toll of friction taken by each *sheave* (pronounced *shiv,* a roller in the block,* or pulley): each sheave exacts about 10 percent of the force applied. The formula gives the relationship of load weight to pull. Any tackle rig can be *rove*

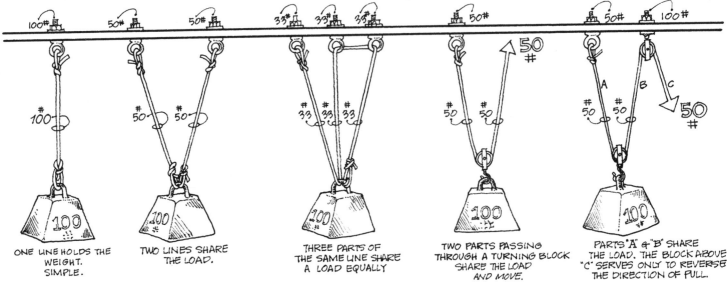

ONE LINE HOLDS THE WEIGHT. SIMPLE.

TWO LINES SHARE THE LOAD.

THREE PARTS OF THE SAME LINE SHARE A LOAD EQUALLY

TWO PARTS PASSING THROUGH A TURNING BLOCK SHARE THE LOAD AND MOVE.

PARTS "A" & "B" SHARE THE LOAD. THE BLOCK ABOVE "C" SERVES ONLY TO REVERSE THE DIRECTION OF PULL.

to *advantage or disadvantage:* the *runner* is rove to advantage because both parts are pulling the moving block; the *whip* uses the block only to change the direction of the pull. In more complex tackle, the number of lines from the moving block, indicates the mechanical advantage.

$$P = \frac{W \,\&\, (\frac{1}{10} \times W)}{ff}$$

P = Pull
W = Weight
S = number of sheaves
ff = number of falls (lines) at the *moving* block

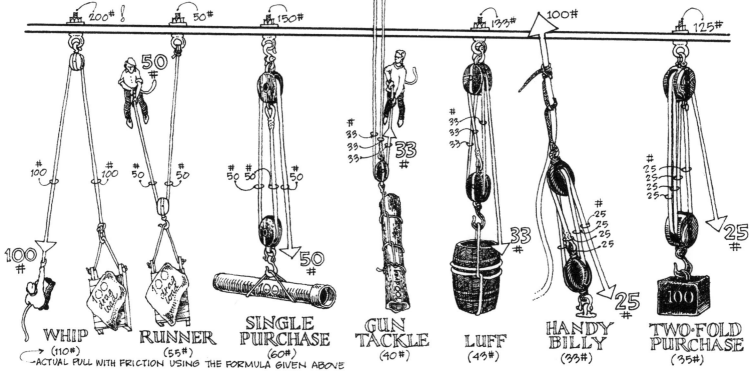

200#   50#   150#   66#   133#   100#   125#

50
#

#   #   #   #   #   #   #   #   #   #   #   #   #   #
100   100   50   50   50 50 50 50   33 33 33 33   33 33 33 33   25 25 25 25

33
#

100
#

50
#

33
#

33
#

25
#

25
#

WHIP   RUNNER   SINGLE   GUN   LUFF   HANDY   TWO·FOLD
                       PURCHASE   TACKLE   BILLY   PURCHASE
(110#)   (55#)   (60#)   (40#)   (43#)   (33#)   (35#)

ACTUAL PULL WITH FRICTION USING THE FORMULA GIVEN ABOVE

33

This sloop is being launched from a beach far from cranes and highlifts, moving on rollers and track and using block & tackle to multiply the pull of a small car in reverse (its most powerful gear). The movers are securing their stationary block to a hefty anchor; ashore, a stationary anchor is called a *dead man*. Sometimes natural dead men aren't available and movers must dig or drill or rig one. The stump puller here is anchored by a well-protected tree. The ground has been dug out as much as possible, and exposed roots have been cut. The tackle has been rove to advantage, the pulling fall on the moving block, and the stump then should come out.

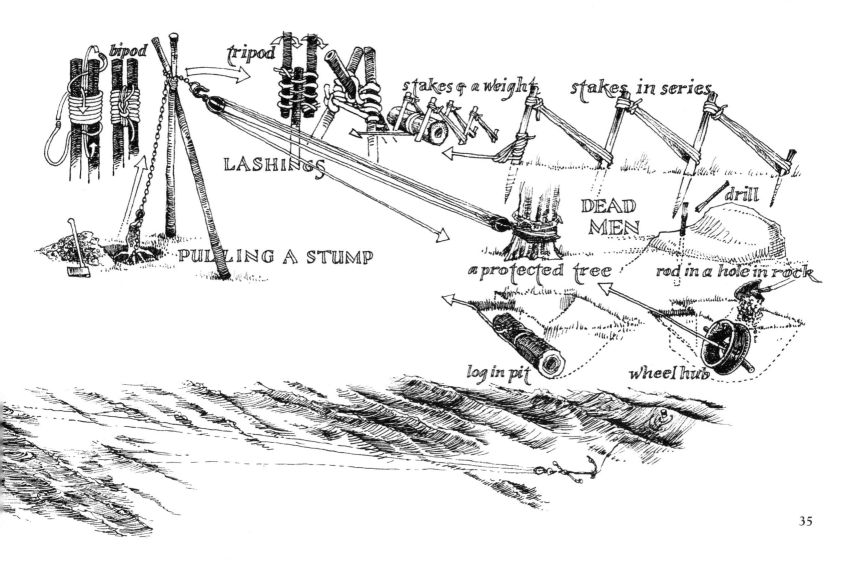

bipod

tripod

stakes & a weight

stakes in series

LASHINGS

DEAD MEN

drill

PULLING A STUMP

a protected tree

rod in a hole in rock

log in pit

wheel hub

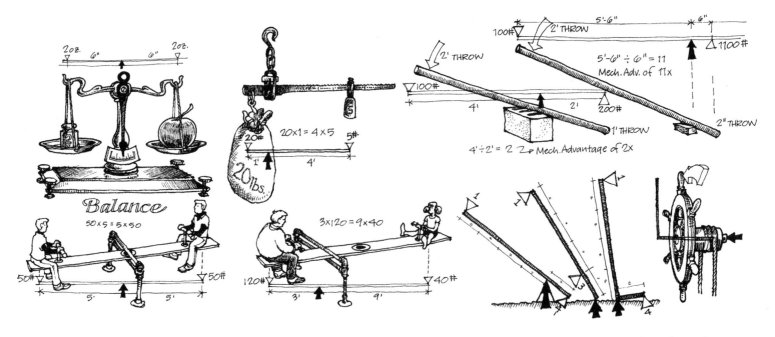

Using levers is a matter of proportion. The force applied on one arm of a lever and the force produced at the other arm are proportional to the lengths of the arms. A balance of equal arms and equal weights is a lever, or a seesaw loaded equally. A seesaw loaded on one side with a person three times as heavy as the other side needs a level arm one-third as long as the light side to strike a balance. The *throws* of the lever arms, the arcs through which they move, are also proportional. If we are content with only a short throw, we can generate enormous force. Levers can be bent and still function: a hand truck is a right-angle lever; the Johnson Bar is a long, angled lifting lever with small wheels; and a wheel can be a double-bend lever, as shown. A lever can be a single arm with the pivot or *fulcrum* at the end. We use levers every day, horizontally and vertically. They are all around us.

36

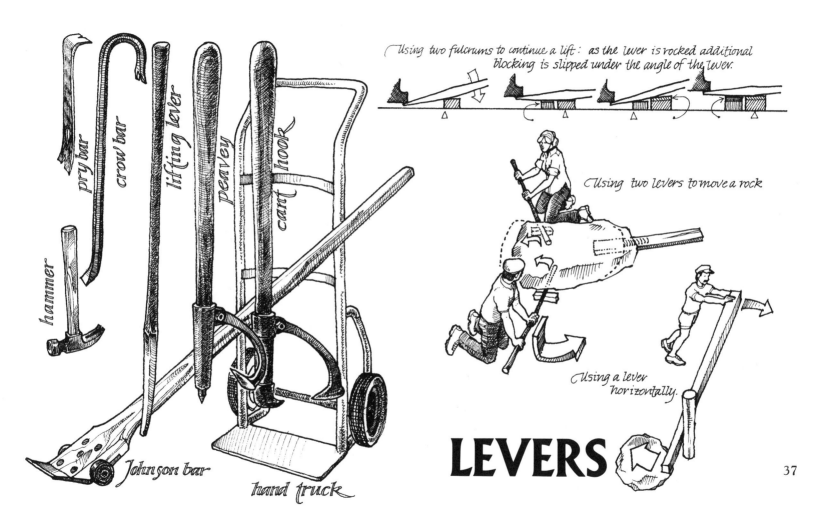

hammer

pry bar

crow bar

lifting lever

peavey

cant hook

Johnson bar

hand truck

Using two fulcrums to continue a lift: as the lever is rocked additional blocking is slipped under the angle of the lever.

Using two levers to move a rock

Using a lever horizontally.

LEVERS

37

WEDGES

The inclined plane, the wedge, must have been the first machine. It was easier to slide a load up a slope than to lift it up a cliff. The little wedge can be a potent tool: the sledgemen at left are launching a ship with wedges. A ship's keel is laid on blocks and the vessel grows with its weight on the ground. When it is complete, a cradle is built in two halves, port and starboard, close to the hull above and resting on greased track below. Thousands of wedges are driven between the track-riding slides of the cradle and the hull-grazing poppets; the wedges force the cradle up to take the weight of the ship off the keel blocks and it is free to slide into the water. Great ships were launched in this basic way and still are.

A tower being lowered by a truck winch goes well for the first sixty degrees, then the horizontal part of the line's pull becomes overwhelming, enough to throw the truck forward, end over end. Something is needed to change the direction of the pull, a *gin pole*, to lower or raise a tall thing like a tower or mast. It can also pull stumps and posts, changing the direction of pull to a nearly vertical angle.

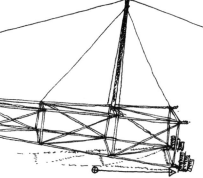

JACKS

To move heavy things you must lift them first. Jacks are designed to convert rotary action or successive levering into vertical motion. Four kinds of jacks are the familiar lever up-and-down car jack, the scissors and screw jack, the tremendously powerful and easily controllable hydraulic jack, and the screw bed jack. Sets of bed jacks are used by house movers, often as back-ups for large hydraulic jacks.

When you are raising anything on a jack, you are perching it on a wobbly pin and creating a perilous situation. Jacks have small bases in proportion to the loads they are lifting, and stability is the first consideration. Movers take major loads up slowly, blocking under any gain of an inch or even less so a shift of the jack isn't a disaster. Their bed jacks and blocking are based foursquare and broad on *cribbing*, parallel pairs of timbers stacked at right angles. By

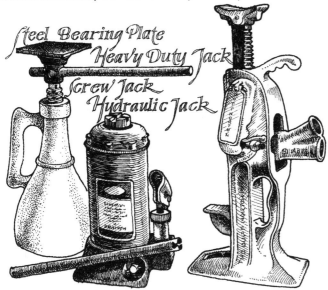

Steel Bearing Plate
Heavy Duty Jack
Screw Jack
Hydraulic Jack

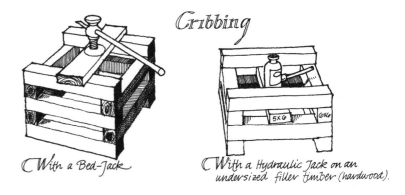

Cribbing

With a Bed-Jack

With a Hydraulic Jack on an undersized filler timber (hardwood).

40

jacking and blocking securely and methodically you can raise houses from foundations or cars from ditches.

To shift a load slightly, movers cant their jacks five or ten degrees *away* from the intended direction of motion. As the jacks assume the weight they rock upright and the burden moves. Mired cars are sometimes moved in the opposite way: one end is jacked up high, brakes are released or chocks are pulled, and the car is pushed *off* the support of the jack toward firm ground. This is a dangerous maneuver; the people who work it stand away from the jack, remove its handle, and usually cross their fingers. The car can probably take the punishment because of its suspension, but you wouldn't want to drop the oil pan on a protruding rock.

One essential piece of equipment doesn't come with your jack: a piece of ⅛″–¼″ steel four or five inches square which seats between jack head and load to distribute force over a broader bearing surface. Because of their shape-assuming bearing surface, inner tubes can be used to lift loads as heavy as engines: they are slipped, deflated, under the engine and then inflated to the proper height.

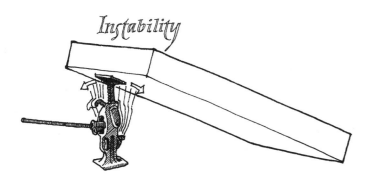

Instability

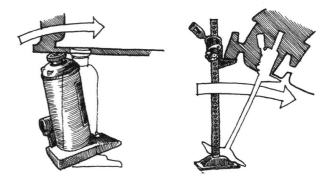

WINCHES

Windlasses and winches range from the traditional *Spanish windlass* (twisting rope to shorten and tighten it) to the sculpture of a double-geared Barient yacht winch (turn the handle clockwise for a mechanical advantage of 12, counterclockwise for an advantage of 24). Powered winches on foredecks and front bumpers are in another class. All winches share the need to apply their enormous forces directly, without side effects. Using a bumper winch at an angle, for instance, can easily flip a truck. The open sided *snatch block* is used to redirect forces.

A drill that comes often to sailors in the intracoastal waterway is *kedging off*, pulling their boat off a grounding. As soon as crew members pick themselves off the deck, one hand rows to deeper water with an anchor while another climbs to the first spreader with a snatch block. The anchor line is

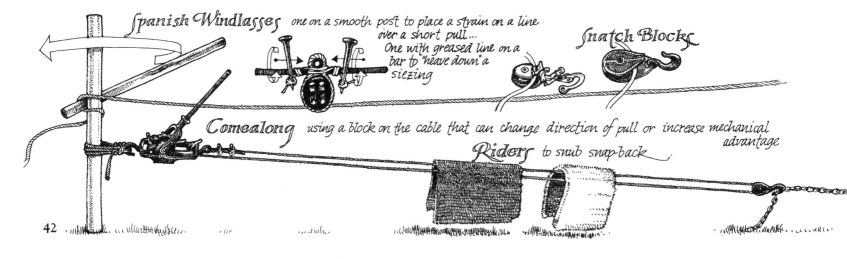

Spanish Windlasses one on a smooth post to place a strain on a line over a short pull... One with greased line on a bar to "heave down" a siezing

Snatch Blocks

Comealong using a block on the cable that can change direction of pull or increase mechanical advantage

Riders to snub snap-back.

led through the snatch block to the windlass on the foredeck, or through an additional snatch block to a sheet winch in the cockpit. As a strain is taken the boat heels (tips), its draft (how deep in the water it sits) is reduced, and it is pulled to safe water. Small boats sometimes accomplish the same thing by attaching the anchor line to a halyard and hauling on the halyard winch, but side pull is hard on the halyard block at the top of the mast.

While they are hauling away at the winch, the crew takes care to keep clear of the line of pull. If the line broke, it would come whipping back with awful force. A faulty line cable or tackle or a worn fitting can let go and send a terrible whip back at the movers. For this reason it is a good practice to drape a few mats or blankets or coats over the strained cable or line of a comealong, winch, windlass, or block & tackle. If anything parts, the air resistance of the riders will limit snap-back, and the effect on the working will be negligible.

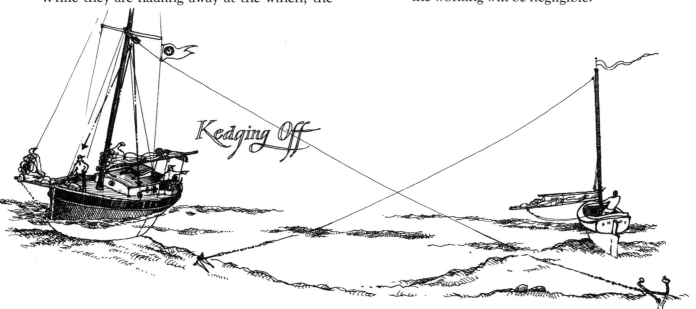

Kedging Off

Everything came in them: soda crackers, bully beef, whale oil, salt, dishes, lobsters, oysters, rum, fish, eggs, and taxidermy specimens. It took a craftsman to make one, but they carried the bulk of shipped goods for this reason: barrels are a magnificent tool for protecting, handling, and moving heavy things. Upright they sit flat and stable and their convex sides present a strong arch to bumps and pressure. Once on their sides a single man can roll huge loads in them, and their convex sides allow him to guide them right or left or spin them into place. They were the first modular containers for cargo, stowing tightly in a ship's hold with built-in

A Quick Flip of crossed hands sets a rolling barrel upright

44

air circulation. Their plain grandchildren, oil drums, are easy to make by machine but not nearly as controllable. Beer kegs, though, stay closer to grandfather's portly shape and are deftly handled because of it.

A few barrel techniques: *parbuckling* uses the round barrel (or drum or pipe or tree trunk) as its own block sheave and offers considerable mechanical advantage with the inclined-plane ramp; learning to flip a barrel upright using its own rolling momentum is almost a dance step, and you had best practice with an empty drum, gloves, and plenty of space first; off loading heavy barrels is easier with an old tire, but watch the jump!

BARRELS

Parbuckling ✳ *Offloading* onto a tire casing ✳ rope & steel *Barrel Tongs* 45

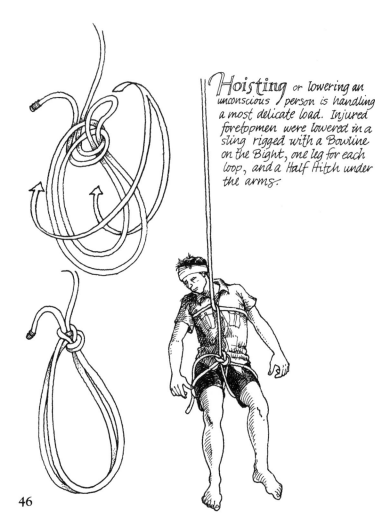

Hoisting or lowering an unconscious person is handling a most delicate load. Injured foretopmen were lowered in a sling rigged with a Bowline on the Bight, one leg for each loop, and a Half Hitch under the arms.

46

Moving heavy things is more a way of thinking than a job. Freshen your eyes, slow down, preen your patience, and get lazy, creatively. It is always surprising how quickly small steps together cover a distance, and how small bids haul a boat into the eelgrass before the sun is over the yardarm. It is mostly a business of putting together plain tools and methods, with a clever trick here or there, to your benefit, and of playing to strengths. Be careful, worry over it a bit, and in all probability you and your friends can leave the cranes and fork lifts to their own loud noises and heave it in place yourselves, if your mind is rove to advantage.

Air bags rolling a pulling boat down a beach.

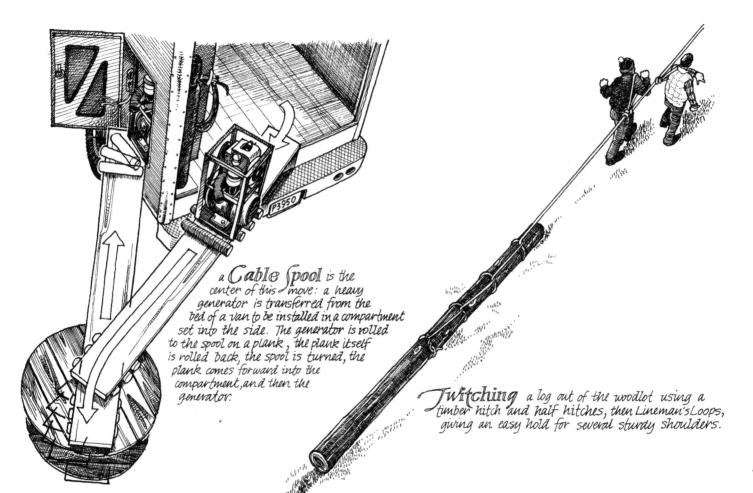

a *Cable Spool* is the center of this move: a heavy generator is transferred from the bed of a van to be installed in a compartment set into the side. The generator is rolled to the spool on a plank, the plank itself is rolled back, the spool is turned, the plank comes forward into the compartment, and then the generator.

Twitching a log out of the woodlot using a timber hitch and half hitches, then Lineman's Loops, giving an easy hold for several sturdy shoulders.

P3950

47

Many friends have given generously to this book, and they have my respectful thanks:

And Friends Moving Company, *whose ability and spirit could move Martha's Vineyard to the other side of Chappaquiddick . . . and may.*

Jay Baldwin, *for technical experience with authority and relish*

John Swain Carter, *the prize of the Peabody*

Bert Bigelow, *for stories and tea*

Dr. Bob Coe, *an observant mariner*

Steve Sperry, *an example*

Skip Warr

Robert Pogany

Buzzard, Inc.

New England Ropes

This volume was set in Goudy Olde Style at Berkeley Typographers, Boston. The display face is Albertus and Albertus Outline.